Fruit in the Garden Clubhouse

Letitia Y. Williams

Self-Discovery Publishing LLC

Visit us on the web:

www.SelfDiscoverySolutions.com

Cover design and illustrations by Nero Gonzaga Bernales, 99Designs 2016

Editing by Susan Walker and Stella Rebecca Michael

ISBN 10: 0-9974831-0-5
ISBN 13: **978-0-9974831-0-9** (paperback)

I dedicate this book to my husband, Bernard. It's a privilege to love, laugh, and live my life with you. I also dedicate it to my mother, Patsy, and the loving memory of my father, Clayborn, who graciously taught me of Jesus Christ's love, which never ceases to bear fruit in my life.

To the people who traveled the road with me—and Sheilah, the one who offered to shave her head! This book was borne of the Lord's decision to interrupt my dance with cancer and bless me with the knowledge to encourage and teach people that the big *C* stands for Christ.

Fruit in the Garden Clubhouse

Contents

Acknowledgments

The Journey

In His infinite wisdom, God blessed me with my mother, Patsy, and my sisters, Jacqueline, Sheilah, and Sherrilyn, who loaded my freezer with chocolate ice cream to comfort my uncertainty. I'm grateful to my brothers-in-law, Neil, Jody, and Sirron, for their words of encouragement and brawn attending to the labor of the land while I recoup. For my nephew Deangelo, I'm thankful he never let the miles between us stand in the way of expressing his love for me. And I send a special heartfelt thank-you to my niece Danica and sister Sherrilyn, for the hours laboring to restore my first dolly, bringing nostalgic memories of my blissful childhood. To my other nieces—Jennifer, Lauren, Kristin, and Sharie—their tender hugs and giggles made the next sunrise promising. To Pastor Bedford and his wife, Victoria, their spiritual support helped me until I again lifted my hands in worship.

Pen to Paper

To my niece Jennifer, I send my deepest appreciation for the many hours of support in the writing of this book. May the love, kindness, and joy you give to others return to you tenfold, and then some! I'm grateful to my biggest supporter, my sister Jacqueline, who has always been my cheerleader, willing to support me no matter the task. Her confidence in me and time invested in this book's completion continues to nudge me toward my highest expectations. My mother showed me what unconditional love feels like with her review of my manuscript. My husband, Bernard, never fails to remind me that life is short: time doesn't wait; if you want it, go get it! Finally, thanks to my illustrator Nero Gonzaga Bernales and editors, Susan Walker and Stella Rebecca Michael, who provided the support to make my vision lift off the pages for my readers.

Chapter 1
The Vine

Once upon a time in a cozy village laced with cobblestone streets, clear blue skies, and the greenest of grass, there lived a young girl named Madison; her father, Roderick; and her mother, Trisha. They were known in this tiny community as the Warren family, and they lived on Swan Lane. Madison was an only child who had few friends but a fantastic imagination. There were many fascinating things in her hometown, but all she really wanted were friends who could play with her and walk the clay-paved road that stretched from one end of the village to the other.

One day at breakfast, Madison asked her parents why there were so few children in their village. Her mother cleared her throat and hesitantly replied, "I overheard the Greens saying a family just bought the house directly behind ours."

Madison's big brown eyes opened wide as she leaped from her chair, dancing and singing with her two long ponytails swaying back and forth. "*Fantastic! Fantastic! Fantastic!* I'll have a best friend after all! My prayers are finally answered." Each morning after that day, before doing anything else, Madison would enthusiastically run to the window to look for the new neighbors. With no success, she'd go downstairs for breakfast before beginning her studies with her mother, who was homeschooling her. After several weeks passed with no new neighbors, Madison started to lose hope and slowly began to feel lonely again.

One sunny afternoon, Madison asked if she could play in the backyard between lessons. Given her freedom, she ran out to the deck and immediately noticed a tiny butterfly. She followed him, hoping they could be friends. She got close enough to see the vibrant yellow and bright orange of his jacket. His wings had tiny white polka dots that reminded her of the cotton balls her mom and dad kept in the bathroom. She laughed, sang, and ran around the yard, trying to catch her new best friend, Mr. Butterfly. Suddenly, the butterfly flew over the fence and out of her view. "Oh no!" she thought. "Don't leave me! This is the most fun I've had in such a long time!" But then Madison heard the sliding door open and her mother calling her in for her math studies, so in she went.

The next couple of days were filled with pouring rain and booming thunder. One night, a loud clatter accompanied a sharp bolt of lightning. Frightened, Madison ran to her parents' room and jumped right between them, where she fell fast asleep. When she awoke, the sun was up and so were her mom and dad. Madison could smell her and her dad's favorite breakfast—corny waffles and sausage. Yum! It was finally Saturday, and this meant shopping in the village to buy lots of stuff from a shop her mom and dad called the "Hole-Stick" (holistic) store. She enjoyed going to the village, but sometimes she didn't want to visit the man they called Doc. He wore a strange gadget around his neck that could hear her heart, and the exam table was very cold. He seemed nice enough, though, so she let him check her tummy. After all, he had the very best lollipops she had ever eaten, and she didn't want to miss out on that!

Later, with the shopping bags loaded in the trunk, they headed home because Madison had grown so tired. On the way, as they drove past the house behind theirs, Madison quickly noticed that someone now seemed to be living there. She saw a shiny red car in the driveway, curtains at the window, and a water hose stretched across the lawn. "Wait! Did I miss the new neighbors moving in?" she thought. Suddenly, she wasn't sleepy; she just wanted to go and investigate.

When they pulled into their own driveway, Madison immediately jumped out of the car and headed toward the backyard. As she pushed open the gate, she felt a big squish. "What on earth is that all over my hands?" she wondered. Grapes were growing in Madison's backyard! Curious, Madison decided to follow the grapes along the fence to see where they would go. The grapes seemed to follow a long branch running along the fence, kind of like a road. Madison walked toward the back of the yard, noticing a hole in the fence just big enough for her to squeeze through. Maybe she should go and see if the new neighbors were home.

She gently poked her head through the hole and saw a girl her age with bright-red hair and medium-brown skin; she was wearing earplugs and sitting in a lawn chair. Madison thought the girl was listening to music, so she called out to her, "Excuse me! Excuse me!" But the girl didn't respond. Madison walked toward the girl, waving her hands and saying hello as she got closer. When the girl looked up, Madison realized she'd been wrong about the earplugs; she saw now that something was covering the girl's mouth and nose.

"Hi! I'm Madison. What's your name?" she asked.

The girl paused for a moment, peering up with the most beautiful green eyes as she pulled a small notebook and a pencil from her pocket and wrote, "I'm Lily. We just moved here from the city. Too much smog." After Madison read the note, Lily wrote, "I'll get into trouble if I have company while taking a treatment. You'd better come back later. My brother will tell on me."

Madison replied, "Okay. I'll come back at five thirty p.m. sharp. There's a little hole in the fence; meet me there."

"For sure!" Lily wrote.

Madison ran home to quickly tell her parents about her new friend. As she made it inside, she was so exhilarated she could hardly speak. With a big smile, Madison took a deep breath and told her parents how thrilled she was to meet Lily. Given all the excitement, Madison and her parents decided to welcome Lily and her family to the neighborhood with a fresh plate of cookies the following day.

"What's that all over your hands and arms?" Madison's dad asked.

"It's grapes. I found them growing on a stick along the fence in the backyard," Madison replied.

"A stick?" both her parents asked her.

"Yep. I found it all by myself," Madison said proudly.

Her parents giggled, and her mom said, "It's not a stick, silly. It's called a grapevine." When Madison asked why, her mom replied, "First things first. Go wash your hands and arms, and I'll share something very special with you after dinner." Quickly the excitement seemed to catch up to Madison all at once, and she suddenly felt very tired. So she washed her hands and lay down for a nap.

A short while later, Madison awoke, full of energy again and ready to play. When the clock read 5:30 p.m., Madison went to the fence, but she didn't see Lily in the backyard. She waited for what seemed like forever, but Lily still didn't come out. Just as she was giving up hope for the day, she heard a tapping noise. She looked over toward the house, and there was Lily in a downstairs window, holding a note. Madison walked over to Lily and saw that the note said, "I can't come out. Mom said your family is coming by tomorrow. See you then! Your friend, Lily." Madison replied with a thumbs-up gesture and a smile, and then off she went back to her house.

That evening, Madison's mother came into her bedroom at bedtime, carrying a book that had pictures of fruit. "Madison, I think you're old enough to learn the story about the grapevine and Jesus Christ." Madison's mother flipped open the book and read from John 15:5: "'I am the vine, you are the branches; he who abides in Me and I in him, he bears much fruit, for apart from Me you can do nothing.' You see, Madison, Jesus is giving us a picture of how much He loves us and how much we need Him. Jesus is just like the grapevine because He supplies all our needs. We are like the grapes, because just as they can't grow without the vine, we can't fully develop without Jesus Christ. Jesus is the vine for us so that we can get nourishment for our bodies and our souls, just like the grapes get nourishment from the grapevine."

Madison was amazed and replied, "Wow! It's awesome that Jesus does this. Is this just for me, Mom?"

Her mom shook her head. "He does it for everyone because He loves us all, and, yes, that includes you, little one. God created the earth and everything in it, so there's nothing He can't do or won't do for us."

With that, Madison knelt down for her bedtime prayers. "I want to tell You something different tonight, Jesus, because I'm so excited about the new friend You sent to me," Madison said. "Thank You for answering my prayers. Thank You for Mommy and Daddy and really thank You for being the vine in my life so I can grow and learn about You and the wonderful things You made. Amen."

The next morning at breakfast, Madison asked, "Mom and Dad, what's up with the grapevine information you told me last night about Jesus? Did Jesus make other yummy fruit in the Bible?"

Her dad smiled and replied, "Actually, yes. Jesus has wonderful lessons on the fruit of the Spirit. Tomorrow we can start teaching them to you. The very first lesson is on love." Then Madison's mom handed her three pills to swallow with her favorite juice before going to church.

Chapter 2
Jesus Is Love

It was Sunday morning, and Madison was excited to visit Lily and her family. Lily would be Madison's first real friend in such a long time. Other kids had come and gone so quickly, some without saying good-bye. Following church, Madison and her mother baked the largest chocolate-chip cookies ever and put twelve on a special plate Madison had chosen to take to Lily's house. Madison's dad came into the kitchen and asked, "Are you girls ready to go for a short visit? The football game is on at three o'clock, and I want to be home in time." Madison and her mother began to laugh; they knew her father wouldn't let anything interfere with football.

"Come on—we're ready!" They piled into the car, and off they went.

Madison pressed the doorbell, setting off a series of soft chimes. The door opened, and there stood a young boy with dark shoulder-length hair, a striped T-shirt, jeans, and a cell phone. "Come on in. I'm Levi. You must be the Warren family that Lily has been talking about."

"Yes," Madison said. "We live in the brown house directly behind you."

Madison and her parents sat in the living room next to a large window. The room was very cozy, with a family portrait hanging over the fireplace. Lily's mother walked into the room, with Lily walking slightly behind her and peeking out at everyone.

"Hello! I'm Carol Peterson," said Lily's mother. "This is Lily, and you've met my son, Levi. My husband, Robert, had to run to the office, but he should be back shortly."

"It's great to meet you," replied Madison's mother. "I'm Trisha. This is my husband, Roderick, and this is our daughter, Madison. We baked you a batch of Madison's favorite chocolate-chip cookies. We hope you like them. They're gluten-free," Trisha said, winking at Carol.

While the parents talked, the girls went to Lily's playroom. The two sat down, played Go Fish, and got to know each other. They shared and laughed, but all too soon, it was time for Madison and her parents to go home. Just before the Warrens left, the parents told the girls that since Lily would be homeschooled as well, their parents had coordinated the girls' break times so they could play in the afternoons.

"Awesome!" the girls said at the same time. "Jinx," they both said, followed by a lot of giggles.

"We noticed the hole in the fence," Carol said. "Robert and I decided to replace the panels with a gate to make visiting a little easier."

"Oh! That's so cool!" cheered Madison as the girls began to laugh again.

"What time can we play tomorrow?" Lily asked.

"Two o'clock," answered Robert, who had returned home from the office.

"See you tomorrow, Madison," Lily said.

"Okay. See you at two o'clock, Lily," Madison replied.

Madison's mother finished making dinner just as the football game was ending. Her dad brought the platter of roasted chicken and mashed potatoes to the table, while her mom grabbed the green peas, dinner rolls, and soft cinnamon butter. The homemade butter was one of Madison's favorites.

"I think we're going to like the Petersons," her mom said. "They seem like a nice family. Don't you think so, Roderick?"

"I do," he replied. "I'm just praying they will be our neighbors for a long time." Then he asked, "Madison, what did you and Lily talk about?"

"Not much. We just talked about games, food, and how glad we are that we live so close and can be friends. I started to ask her about the thing she had on her face the day I saw her in the backyard, but since we'll be friends forever, I'll ask her later," Madison said.

"What 'thing'?" her dad asked.

"The first day I saw her, she had something on her face covering her nose and mouth," Madison explained. "She called it a treatment, but I'm not sure what that is."

"Well, I'm sure she'll tell you when she's ready," her mother said. "How are you feeling today?" her mother asked.

"I feel a little tired, but I'm not really sleepy," Madison replied. "My

tummy was hurting earlier in church. I decided to wait to tell you because I didn't want you to keep me home from meeting Lily."

In a stern voice, her dad scolded her, saying, "That's unacceptable, Madison! If you're not going to tell us when you're feeling sick, you will not be able to visit Lily. Do you hear me?"

With tears brimming in her brown eyes, she said, "Yes. I'm sorry; I won't do it again." She sniffled and then pleaded, "Can I please still play with her tomorrow?"

"Well, Madison, what your father really means is that we can't help you feel better when we don't know that something is wrong," her mother explained. "Remember the story about Jesus being the vine to us just as the grapevine is to the grapes? Because we're your parents, Jesus gives us things that we can do to help you if you're not feeling well. It's very important that you tell us right away," her mom explained.

"Okay. I promise! I promise!" Madison vowed.

That night, after having a warm cookie with her dad and then a bubble bath, Madison put on her favorite pj's. They were pastel pink with four bunnies on the front. She loved them because they were so incredibly soft and because they didn't have a seam that would brush against the scar on her tummy.

"Madison, you had a very full day today, and tomorrow will be your first playdate with Lily," her mom said. "Are you excited?"

"Oh yes, Mommy! I can't wait to talk to her again!" Madison said.

"That's my girl, the socialite—always wanting to meet people," her mom teased. Madison beamed in response.

"Let's read the next fruit story about Jesus before saying our prayers," her mom said as she opened the book. "Remember when I explained that Jesus is the vine in our life, much like the grapevine is to the grapes?" her mom asked. "Well, Jesus also has ways that we can show other people we love Him through our actions. These actions are called the fruit of the Spirit."

"Really? Does that mean I can act like an apple head?" Madison asked, giggling.

"No, silly, not an apple head," her mom answered, smiling. "The Bible teaches us that Jesus named nine actions that we can take to show others that we love Him and have Jesus in our heart. These nine things are called the fruit of the Spirit. The first fruit of the Spirit is love."

"So when I show someone that I love them, I'm acting like Jesus?" Madison asked.

"Yep—that's it, Madison. The Bible explains it to us. 1 John 3:18 says, 'Little children, let us not love with word or with tongue, but in deed and truth.'"

"So when I show people that I love them, that's how God lives in me?" Madison asked to clarify.

"Yes, dear daughter, that's how it's done," her mom said.

"How do I know if I'm showing someone that I love them?" Madison asked.

Her mother read on. "As the Bible tells us in 1 Corinthians 13:4, 'Love is patient, love is kind and is not jealous; love does not brag and is not arrogant.'"

"Mom, you and Dad are patient and kind with me when I don't feel well," said Madison.

"Yes," her mother replied. "You're right. You're our little angel, and we love you. And so does Jesus. He made you from the top of your head to the tip of your toes, and He made everything in between too." Her mom tickled Madison.

"Do you think Jesus knows that I don't always feel well?" Madison questioned.

"Yes, He does, and that's why He gave you to us, so that we can take care of you when you don't feel well," her mom reassured her.

Madison yawned and said, "He's the greatest. Can we say our prayers now?" Her mother placed a kiss on her forehead, and then Madison and her mom knelt down by the side of her bed. Madison prayed, "Dear Jesus, I love You so much that I want to share my homemade chocolate-chip cookies with You so that You have a special treat too. Thank You for Mommy, Daddy, Lily, Levi, and their mom and dad too. I love You. Amen."

Chapter 3
Joy to the World

Lunch was finally over on Monday afternoon, which meant it was time to play with Lily. Madison and her mother walked onto the deck just in time to see Robert putting the final screws on the back gate that joined their yards. When he saw them, he waved and chuckled. "Come and check out the magic door," he invited.

As they got closer, they saw Lily sitting in the grass, wearing a soft yellow short set with a gray-and-white kitten print. "That's a really cute outfit," Madison said.

"Thanks," replied Lily. "I like yours too."

Madison turned to her mother and asked, "Is this a loving action, as Jesus would like us to do?" Her mother nodded in approval.

Lily asked, "What's that?"

"I'll tell you later," Madison said. "Let's go play!"

Trisha thanked Robert for putting in the gate so quickly for the girls and then headed back home. Madison and Lily tossed the sticks that were piled in the corner of Lily's yard. "Hey, Dad," Lily called, "can you help us build a fort?"

Robert checked his watch and said, "I can't right now. I need to run to work for a bit. Maybe I can help you tomorrow."

"All right," Lily responded in a low tone. Then she brightened and said, "I've got an idea! Let's get Levi to help us today!"

The girls ran inside and up the stairs, calling, "Levi! Levi! Where are you?"

Suddenly, Lily got very still and said, "Go get my dad—right now!"

Madison ran down the steps, yelling, "Mr. Peterson, Mr. Peterson! It's Lily! Come quick!"

Robert rushed in past Madison and up to the step where Lily was standing and panting. With one whisk, he swept her from her feet and took her to a nearby room. He quickly strapped something over her nose and mouth, and it seemed to help her breathe.

As he rocked Lily back and forth, Madison began to pray aloud, "Jesus, please make my friend, Lily, well. She's such a nice person, and I want her to be well so that we can be friends forever. And, Jesus, please help Mr. Peterson to know how to show her the love she needs, just like You show Mom and Dad how to help me when I'm sick. Thank You, Jesus. I love You. Amen."

In amazement, Mr. Peterson called, "Levi! Levi! Come here, now!"

"Yeah, Dad. What's up?" Levi asked.

"Why don't you walk Madison home? Her mother is in the den and will see you when you go through the new back gate," Robert said.

"Bye, Lily. I hope you feel better soon," said Madison.

As Madison and Levi approached the sliding door of her house, her mother came out and asked, "Is everything all right, Levi?"

"It's Lily," Levi answered. "She had an asthma attack, so my dad asked me to walk Madison home. Maybe they can play later."

"Okay. Thank you," she replied. "Please tell your father to let me know if I can help."

"Sure. Thank you," replied Levi, before he ran back to the gate.

With tear-filled eyes, Madison asked, "Did I do something wrong, Mom? Do you think her dad is mad at me?"

"Of course he isn't mad at you, Madison," Trisha assured her. "I'm sure you didn't do anything wrong. It's just that Lily can't run and jump a lot. When you two play, try to do something that's calm. Okay?"

"Sure," said Madison. "Well, Mom, I prayed for Lily to get better, and I believe Jesus will make her well."

"Good girl, Madison," her mom said. "You've had a full day. Let's take the rest of the afternoon off from your studies. We can call Lily later to check on her. Okay?" her mom said as she rubbed Madison's back to calm her.

"Thanks, Mom. You're the best," said Madison.

A couple of hours later, Trisha called Robert to check in. "How is Lily?" she asked.

"She's doing okay now," Robert said. "I think she got too excited and had an asthma attack. Sometimes she gets so exhausted after an attack that I just let her nap."

"Well, we are here if you need anything," Trisha said. "Don't hesitate to call on us, and be sure to tell Lily that Madison hopes she'll be better soon."

"Sure. Will do. Thanks again," Robert said as he hung up the phone.

Trisha felt odd after the call to Robert, but she couldn't put her finger on what exactly made her uneasy, so she just put it out of her mind.

Later that evening, Madison's dad called her into the room and said, "I'm going to read your bedtime story tonight and give Mom a little break, if that's okay with you."

"Of course," said Madison as she settled on his lap. "What are you going to read me?"

Her dad opened up the book with the fruit and said, "We are going to continue to read about Jesus and the fruit of the Spirit. In addition to love, the Bible tells us that joy is also a teaching of Jesus Christ."

"How so, Dad?" she asked.

"Well, Madison, Christ teaches us about His joy with the scripture from 1 Thessalonians, chapter 5. It says, 'Rejoice always; pray without ceasing; in everything give thanks; for this is God's will for you in Christ Jesus.'"

"Are you sure Jesus wants us to have joy?" she questioned.

"Yes. The Word of Christ teaches that the joy of the Lord is our strength," her father explained.

Madison thought about that for a moment before asking, "So when I'm joyful, even when I don't feel good, because I know Jesus is in my heart, then that's His strength in me?"

"Yep! That sure is, Madison," he replied. "And He makes that strength available for all of us. He loves us so much. The teachings of Jesus only get better and better."

"Oh, fantastic! I can hardly wait to learn more. Can I pray and thank Him now?" asked Madison.

"Yes, you sure can," he said with a smile.

Madison climbed down from her father's lap. She then knelt at the side of her bed and bowed her head. Then she opened her eyes and gently reached out her hand, saying, "Dad, I love you. Come kneel with me while I pray." The two of them together held hands in complete silence. Finally, Madison took a deep breath and prayed, "Jesus, I love You so much and really want to thank You for letting me find strength when I need it most. And I also feel joyful most of the time, and I didn't know that's because You're in my heart. So don't be mad at me for not knowing it was You all the time. I promise to make sure other people know that they can make You happy by loving others. Thank You for Mom and Dad. I'm really glad You took care of Lily today when she was sick. I'll talk to You tomorrow. Amen."

Her father opened his eyes, which were filled with tears of joy, and kissed Madison on her forehead. "I have the most treasured daughter in the world," he said, "and I thank Jesus every day for you."

"Do you really, Dad? Or are you just saying that?" she asked with a smile.

"No. I'm not just saying it. I mean it, really," her dad said. "Now get some sleep." He turned off her lamp.

"Good night, Mom. I'll see you tomorrow," Madison called out.

Chapter 4
Peace upon Us

The day seemed to move along at a normal pace, with nothing much out of the norm. Madison wondered how Lily was doing, because it had been several days since her asthma attack. Trisha decided to call Robert and Carol to see how things were going. Carol answered the phone, and to Trisha's surprise, she seemed a little distant. Trisha asked if everything was okay, and she said yes but that Lily wasn't up to a playdate just yet, possibly in a day or two. Trisha offered to help if she could. Carol thanked her and declined.

"Mom," Madison asked, "can I make a craft today for my art class?"

"Yes. In fact, it's time for that now. C'mon, let's get artsy!" Trisha walked into the kitchen and took out the art supplies and paper towels.

"Mom, what are the rules that I have to follow today for my art project?" Madison asked.

"Well, I was thinking that you could do something related to the fruit of the Spirit that you've been learning about," her mom replied.

"Can I make it into a get-well card for Lily, too?" Madison asked.

"Okay. That would be very nice," her mom replied.

Madison folded a piece of construction paper in half, took out a brown crayon, and began to draw what appeared to be a long and winding line all over the front cover. She then opened the folded paper and continued to draw inside of it as well. Madison grabbed the purple crayon and, on the front of the card, wrote, "I hope you get well soon. Follow this vine, and see what you get." She then opened the card and began to make small purple circles every so often along the line. At the end, she made a circle larger than the others. Inside the card, she wrote, "Jesus is the vine in our life, and He supplies all our needs. Just believe in His word, and everything will be all right." She signed the card, "Love, your friend, Madison."

Her mother couldn't have been prouder than she was in that moment, for she knew that Madison's love for the Lord was shining through as she shared her love, joy, and faith with her dear friend, Lily.

"Madison, you're such a smart girl," her mom said. "I think we should discuss the next fruit of the Spirit right now."

"Well, I usually say my prayers after and go to bed. Does that mean I'll have to go to bed right after?" Madison asked.

"No, of course not," her mom said, laughing.

"What about my prayers? I may forget something if I have to wait until tonight," Madison said.

"You don't ever have to wait to pray or talk with Jesus, Madison. He is available whenever you need Him," her mom explained.

"Awesome! Let's get to the next fruit of the Spirit."

As her mom pulled out the book with the fruit, she said, "The Bible is the Lord's Word, and I'm going to read you what it says about peace. The book of Romans 5:1 states, 'Therefore, having been justified by faith, we have peace with God through our Lord Jesus Christ.'"

"What does that mean, Mom?" Madison asked.

"It means that when we have faith in God, He gives us peace, especially with the things that trouble or upset us. Maybe this next passage will help to clear things up for you, Madison. The book of John 16:33 also says, 'These things I have spoken to you, so that in Me you may have peace. In the world you have tribulation, but take courage; I have overcome the world.' You see, Madison, we can find our peace in Jesus, and then the challenges we experience don't seem so bad because Jesus already knows all about them."

"He's already taken care of them too?" asked Madison.

"Yes, He has."

"Okay, with that good news, can I make Dad a picture, too?" asked Madison. When her mom said she could, Madison grabbed a sheet of paper and began to make a landscape with long blades of green grass. She added a barn in the background and a bright sun in the sky, and then she made daisies throughout the grass.

"What are they?" her mother asked.

"You're silly, Mom. Can't you tell they're daisies, my favorite flower?" said Madison.

"Of course, I can tell, Madison. What I'm wondering is why some are larger than others," her mom replied.

"Well, the larger daisies are the ones that have faith, so they are full and running over with peace and joy. The smaller ones do not have faith, but because Jesus loves them, they can one day be filled with peace and joy. They just have to believe in Jesus first to have this special kind of peace and joy. That's why I made them smaller than the others," Madison explained.

Mom looked at her in amazement. "You got all that from the fruit of the Spirit, Madison?"

"Yes. Is that right?" Madison asked.

"You bet it's right! You're so easy to teach! I love you," her mom said.

Suddenly, Madison said, sighing, "Mom, I think I'm getting tired. Can we stop now?"

"Yes, dear. Go wash your hands, and go to the den. I'll bring you a snack to have with your afternoon meds."

Chapter 5
Patience beyond Measure

Trisha called Carol and Robert to see if Lily could come over for a playdate, but she did not get an answer. She'd promised Madison they could put Lily's card in her mailbox when they came from visiting Doc. When they arrived at Madison's appointment, something seemed a little different from other visits. Maybe it was because Dad was at work and Madison and her mother were alone this time. Doc's waiting room even seemed smaller, or perhaps just more crowded than usual. While waiting their turn, Madison overheard someone saying that it's hard to look at so many with the big *C*.

"'What on earth was that?" Madison wondered. "Do I have that? Does everyone have the big *C*?" She was determined to find out what this meant. After a long wait, the nurse called them to a room where they met with Doc. He asked a lot of questions about how she had been feeling, and he wanted to hear all about her tummy aches. When they finished, Doc told Trisha to take Madison to have an x-ray to peek inside her tummy.

"Thanks, Doc, for helping me. You must really love Jesus, since you are helping all those sick people in your lobby who have the big *C*," said Madison.

Surprised, Doc responded, "Thank you, Madison. In fact, I do love Jesus, and He has made it possible for me to learn how to be a good doctor so I can help people when they don't feel well. That's one way that I show His love through my actions."

With a big smile, Madison said, giggling, "Okay. Now can I have one of those suckers?"

"Sure! Grab two on the way out because you're extra special," said Doc.

As they walked through the lobby, Madison spotted Lily and her parents. Lily's mother looked sad. Madison walked over to Lily and told her she would have a surprise in her mailbox when she got home. "Call me to let me know what you think of it," Madison said.

This news seemed to lift Lily's spirits; her big green eyes opened a little wider, and a big grin spread over her face. "Okay! For sure I'll call you as soon as I see it." Then she whispered excitedly, "Hey, I was thinking, since I can't really do much running, maybe we could build a private clubhouse near the gate! That way we could both use it. What do you think, Madison? It could be like our own little house."

"A clubhouse sounds like fun," Madison said. "But who will help us build it?"

"I've been thinking about that too," whispered Lily. "It just so happens that Levi owes me a big favor because I covered for him last week. I should be able to get him to build it for us."

"When do you think we can do this?" asked Madison.

"I'll know more after my appointment today," replied Lily. "Call you later, Madison."

"For sure! Bye, Lily!" said Madison.

By late afternoon, Madison kept wondering if Lily had liked the get-well card she'd left for her. As the sun began to set, she knew it would soon be bedtime, and she really wanted to talk with Lily. Suddenly, she heard the phone ring. She dashed across the room and grabbed the phone, saying, "Lily?"

"It's me all right. I like the card! Thank you so much. I have it on my dresser. I don't really understand everything you wrote, so you'll have to tell me what you meant."

"Okay," Madison said.

We can talk about it in our clubhouse," Lily said softly.

"Did Levi say he would do it?" asked Madison.

Lily giggled and whispered, "Yes. He's going to make it tomorrow while Dad is gone to work. That way he can't say no! If you don't mind, he'll put it under the orange tree; it'll be out of the way, and Dad shouldn't care."

"Okay! Call me tomorrow when you go out," Madison said, "and I'll see if I can come over for a while."

"All right. I'll call you then. Good-bye!" said Lily.

Madison hung up the phone and went back into the living room. Just then, her mom came in the room holding two bowls of vanilla ice cream topped with caramel sauce. Her mother handed Madison her treat, and they both settled on the couch. She said, "Madison, I want to share something with you. Tonight, I thought I'd read to you from the book of Ephesians 4:2 on patience, another fruit of the Spirit. What I'm most proud about tonight is that you've already been using this gift, and that makes me so very happy. The Bible says we should act this way concerning patience. It says, 'With all humility and gentleness, with patience, showing tolerance for one another in love.' The way I saw you care for Lily today at the doctor's office really made me proud to have you as my daughter."

"Aw...thanks, Mom. That's so sweet. Maybe I should get more ice cream?" Madison said, giggling. As they finished up their cool treat, Trisha noticed that Madison was already beginning to fall asleep; she gently took her dish and rested Madison's head on her lap. Then she curled up, too.

Chapter 6
Kindness

A tapping rhythm woke Madison up. Her mom must have brought her to bed, since she wasn't on the couch anymore. Madison climbed out of bed and peeked through her bedroom blinds. Levi was in the yard, building the clubhouse for Madison and Lily. Madison could hardly contain her excitement. She went to tell her mother and father, but they weren't in their bedroom or the kitchen. "Have they left me here alone?" she wondered. As she walked into the den, she heard the front door close. "Mom? Dad? Is that you?"

"Sleepyhead, you finally woke up," her mother said, holding the mail in one hand.

Madison ran toward her mom's voice, greeting her with a big hug. "Mom! Mom!" she said as she tugged on her mother's top. "Levi is building me and Lily a clubhouse so we can play quietly in the yard."

"Oh, how wonderful, Madison! Are Lily's parents okay with that?"

"I guess so, since Levi is doing it," Madison said.

"Let's go and have a look," her mom said. "But first, you have to brush your teeth, put on your robe, and have some breakfast."

"Okay!" Madison replied as she ran off.

When she returned to the kitchen, it looked as if her mother had been crying.

"Are you okay?" Madison asked. "You look like you're crying."

"Oh, Madison...I didn't see you standing there," she said. "Yes, I'm fine. Look, I made you pancakes for breakfast. You finish eating, and then we'll look at the clubhouse before going to see Doc. He called to make an appointment for you."

Madison finished her breakfast. Just as she was putting her glass and plate in the sink, her mother came in with her morning pills and said, "You can swallow these with the rest of the milk you were going to dump down the drain."

Madison giggled as she reached for the pills and said with a smile, "I wasn't going to do that!"

Madison and her mother finished up in the kitchen and went outside to the see the clubhouse. They opened the gate and found Levi nailing wooden boards together. Madison ran over to him and said, "Levi, you're the best brother ever! This is great!"

"Thanks. I'm trying to get it done before Lily and Mom come back from the doctor's office, and definitely before Dad gets home from work. He's so particular about his lawn," Levi said, shrugging his shoulders with a smile. "It will be up today, so feel free to come back later. Lily should be home in a couple of hours."

"Okay. Thanks, Levi!" Madison said. "You're the greatest!"

Madison and her mom left for their appointment with Doc. When they arrived at the hospital, they were shown to a small waiting room. The nurse gave Madison a gown to wear for the x-ray. While they waited, they watched a cartoon called *The Flintstones*. Her mom explained that this show had been her favorite cartoon when she was a kid. The big guy, Fred, and his dinosaur were very funny.

They had been waiting awhile, when, suddenly, the door to the room opened, and in walked Lily, holding her mother's hand. Lily's mom was sobbing.

"Lily? What's wrong?" asked Madison, running over to her.

Lily blurted out that she may have cancer again.

"What's that?" Madison asked.

Lily shrugged. "I don't know for sure," she said, "but it can really hurt a lot."

"Oh no! Lily, we have to tell Jesus about it. He can help no matter what the problem is," Madison said, giving Lily a big hug.

Lily started to follow her mom into the changing room but then abruptly pulled away from her and turned back to Madison. She asked, "Madison, do you have the big *C* too?"

Madison, reacting with confusion and panic, asked, "What? The big *C*?

Is that cancer? Is that why I'm here? Is that why I take all these pills and sleep a lot? Am I going to hurt because of it?"

Carol, with a look of horror, picked up Lily and said, "You don't ask people about personal things! I'm sure Madison is going to be fine." Carol looked at Trisha, and as their eyes met, they knew they'd need to discuss it later.

Just then a nurse came in for Madison. "Come on, dear," the nurse said. "We're going to have a peek, and then you'll be back home in no time." As the three of them walked down the hall, Madison couldn't help but wonder what was wrong with her. Had her parents been keeping a secret from her, that she had some big *C* too?

A short time later, Madison and her mom came back to the waiting room. "The nurse was nice," she told her mom. "I lay on my back and kept very still, and in no time I was all done. No pain at all!"

The car ride home was quieter than usual. Finally, Madison asked the question that had been on her mind since seeing Lily. "Mom, do I have the big *C* that Lily was talking about?"

"We don't know that, Madison," her mom answered. "But I can tell you this—no matter what, you're going to be just fine. Don't spend another minute thinking about it. In fact, I have a great idea. Let's do some shopping for your new clubhouse." They returned home with art supplies to decorate, a small plastic table with four orange chairs, and two big waterproof floor pillows. One pillow was green and the other a bright yellow.

When things finally slowed down, it was late afternoon, and Madison was anxious to see the clubhouse and show Lily their new things. Anticipating this, her mom said, "Madison, I have a sneaky feeling that you'll want to play for a while, so let's work on one lesson before I call Carol. Your choice. What's it going to be? Math maybe?"

Madison yelled, "No! Not math! Let's learn another fruit."

"Another fruit? Oh, you mean the next fruit of the Spirit. Well, first of all, they aren't actual fruits—not like an apple or a peach," her mother explained. "They are attributes that teach us how Christians are to live."

"What's an *att-ti-tue*?" Madison asked, laughing.

Her mom chuckled too and said, "That's *attribute,* and an attribute is a quality. The fruit of the Spirit is a biblical term that teaches us the nine visible traits about living a Christian life."

"So because I believe in Jesus Christ, I should use these attributes in my actions so people will know I am Christian?" Madison asked.

"Yes," her mom said, "but more importantly, using them shows that God loves you, and with His love in your heart, you're able to love others and share with them." When Madison nodded with understanding, her mom continued. "The next fruit of the Spirit is kindness."

"Oh, I know how to be kind to others, but what does Jesus say about it?" asked Madison.

Reading from the book of Ephesians 4:32, her mom said, "The Bible says, 'Be kind to one another, tender-hearted, forgiving each other, just as God in Christ also has forgiven you.'"

Madison mulled over this idea. "Mom, does this mean that I should be kind to everyone and teach them about Jesus?"

"Yes. I think that would make Him very happy," her mother replied.

"Cool! I've got it, and I know what I have to do. Could you please call Lily's mother now?" Madison asked.

Chapter 7
Only Goodness

Madison's mother phoned Lily's mother, and Madison waited anxiously for someone to answer.

"Hello. This is Lily. Who's this?"

"Hi, Lily," Madison's mom said. "This is Trisha. Is your mom home?"

"Yep. Hold on," Lily said. "I'll go get her."

"Hello, Trisha. It's Carol. How did things go for you?" she asked.

"If you have some time, I could come over to talk. Madison is bugging me about the new clubhouse," Trisha answered.

"Lily's bugging me, too," Carol said. "Why don't you come on over now, if you're free? And, Trisha, use the back fence. It's not just for the kids!" Carol laughed.

Trisha laughed too. "Yes, I will. See you in fifteen."

A few minutes later, Madison and her mom were knocking on their neighbors' door. "Carol, it's Trisha and Madison here for a little visit," Trisha called out through the screen door.

"Come on in!" Carol yelled. "The door is unlocked for you. I'm making us a pot of coffee, so come to the kitchen."

Lily met them at the door. The girls left giggling as Lily led Madison out to the clubhouse. Trisha sat down at the counter. Carol came over to her and, with a warm, tearful hug, said, "I'm so sorry you're going through this too. I didn't realize Madison was unaware of her circumstances. Maybe with Lily being a year older, she's picked up on more about her situation."

"We've tried to keep her knowingly distant from it because she is just so young," Trisha said. "But clearly Roderick and I need to have a conversation with Madison. We would rather she hear about her circumstances from us than anyone else."

"I agree with you on that," Carol said. "So how do you keep Madison encouraged? She has to know something is going on."

"We are wrapping her up in the love of Jesus so that when she does know, she will already have her faith to help her work through any challenges she encounters," Trisha replied.

"That's interesting," Carol said. "Robert and I don't really go to church or anything, but we do know of God. There's just one question I keep asking myself. Why did He choose Lily for this?"

Trisha placed a hand on Carol's shoulder and said, "Oh Carol, I understand what you mean, but Jesus is not disciplining our girls or wanting to see them hurt. He's designed their life with a much bigger purpose. And while I can't explain everything, I know for certain that He has allowed this disease to play out in their lives for there to be sunshine after this storm. You just have to believe, submit, and trust in Him as your Lord and Savior, Carol. He's over all of this, so find comfort in knowing He's got this all worked out."

Carol held back her tears as she replied, "Oh Trisha, how badly I want to believe that, but I just don't know how. I need to know that no matter what, my baby is going to be okay."

"I've got an idea," said Trisha. "The girls can get together each day as part of their studies, and we can study the Word of Jesus Christ too. We can start tomorrow morning, if you'd like. How about eleven o'clock?"

Carol smiled and said, "I'd like that. Now, let's check on our girls. They are awfully quiet."

As the moms made their way across the yard, they could hear the laughter and joy of the two girls. "Oh, Mom, look at what Madison and her mom bought for the clubhouse!" Lily said with excitement.

"Oh my! Do I owe you anything for this, Trisha?" Carol asked.

"Nope. You'll have the noise most of the time. It's the least I could do," Trisha replied. They laughed and hugged, for they knew they had found a friend, just as their girls had. "We're going to head home in fifteen minutes, Madison, so start wrapping it up," Trisha said as she headed back inside with Carol.

When Madison and her mom got back to their house, her dad was in the kitchen making sandwiches for dinner. "How are you feeling, Madison?" he asked.

"I feel a little tired, but mostly okay," she replied.

Her mother prepped dinner trays for the three of them so they could eat in the family room on their fluffy floor pillows. After saying grace, her dad said, "So, Madison, today you asked what was meant by the big *C*, and we would like to tell you what that means. The *C* stands for cancer, although we prefer to think of it as the little *c*, because the big *C* in this house stands for Christ—Jesus Christ! We call Him the big *C* because we know that Jesus Christ is over all things, and we are always safe with Him. When you were a little tot, the doctors discovered you had a rare kind of cancer, so we took you to see a specialist to decide what to do. The doctor was able to remove the cancer, and that's why you have the scar on your tummy. We know you'll be fine, but we have to keep a check to make sure it doesn't come back and that you stay healthy and strong. Do you have any questions?"

"Why do I have this cancer?" Madison asked.

"We don't know why, honey," her mom replied, "but we know the Lord has made many treatments available to help you and the other children who are faced with this situation. We moved here for the clean air to breathe, which is a tremendous help."

"So am I going to be all right?" Madison asked.

"Of course you are, Madison," her dad said. "But that's why we see Doc and shop at the holistic shops to buy you the very best our money can afford."

With a big hug, Madison said, "Thanks, Mom and Dad, for loving me so much. But what's Jesus saying about all this?"

Mom replied, "He's guiding us on how to care for you, just as He guides the many other parents who have similar situations. You see, Madison, in Galatians 6:9, the Bible talks about goodness. It says, 'Let us not lose heart in doing good, for in due time we will reap if we do not grow weary.' So, as a family, let's stay in faith, pray about this, and continue to do good, according to the Lord's will." She continued, saying, "By the way, Madison, goodness is a fruit of the Spirit."

"Let's use this visible trait or *att-ti-tue*," Madison said hesitantly, "to show that Jesus lives in us."

"That's the best recommendation I've heard all week," her dad said, kissing her on the forehead.

Chapter 8
His Faithfulness

Madison couldn't tie her shoelaces quickly enough in anticipation of her visit with Lily. While Madison fussed with her shoes, Trisha went to close the garage door. On the way, she spotted a large bell on a corner shelf. When Madison appeared in the doorway, she saw her mother taking the bell down and asked why.

"If Carol is okay with it," she explained, "we can mount it on the fence for a doorbell."

"Great idea!" Madison agreed with a smile.

They arrived to find Carol and Lily excited to spend time together on this warm spring day. The girls headed across the backyard to the clubhouse as Trisha and Carol went inside with the bell.

"Do you want to decorate the clubhouse today?" Lily asked.

"Yes, and I have the perfect plan," Madison said. Madison began to explain that up above in heaven, there's a wonderful man named Jesus Christ. He has many talents, and He keeps watch over the entire world. We could decorate using Jesus Christ as our inspiration.

Lily couldn't imagine anyone having more power than the tooth fairy, the Easter bunny, and Santa. "How come I don't know about all this?" she asked.

"I don't know," Madison replied. "But I know He is really good to us. It's because of Him and His goodness that moms and dads all over the world are able to be good to their kids."

"Wow! How awesome is that!" Lily said. "Can I get Mom put on punishment when she doesn't give me a second dessert?"

Madison laughed. "I'm not sure. I haven't tried that. But you can certainly tell Him what's going on at any time, because He doesn't sleep and is always willing to talk to us."

Lily thought about this plan for a moment and then told Madison, "I don't know much about Jesus. How will I know what to put on the walls?"

Madison replied, "Let's decorate our clubhouse with the fruit of Spirit. That way, we'll be reminded of how Jesus wants us to act whenever we play here."

"What are fruit of the Spirit?" Lily asked.

"I was confused at first, too," Madison replied. "They are visible traits that show other people that Jesus lives in our hearts. The fruit of the Spirit has nine actions that we can take. We can do some of them even if we don't believe, but when we really believe..." Madison paused and then, a second later, said, "Watch out—big things can happen! After all, Jesus made us, the world, and everything in it. Here are the fruit of the Spirit actions I know about. There's love, joy, peace, patience, kindness, and goodness."

"How do we draw all that?" asked Lily.

"Let's start with the vine, since Jesus is to us as the grapevine is to the grape. Without the vine, you have no life," Madison explained.

The next couple of hours were full of laughter and hard work as the girls decorated the clubhouse with the warm love of Jesus. But then, all of a sudden, Madison felt a sharp pain and told Lily that she needed to go home. The girls went inside, and Trisha walked Madison home for medication and a nap.

Madison awoke to find the sun setting for the day. "Mom, are we going back to the clubhouse?" Madison asked.

"No, not tonight. We will see our friends tomorrow for lunch and a playdate," her mom said.

"I think I'm hungry," Madison said. "What's for dinner?"

"Your dad and I ate already, but your plate is in the kitchen. I'll read you a passage from the Bible while you enjoy dinner." Madison washed her hands and sat down for a bowl of chicken and dumplings.

"Today, Madison," her mom began, "we are going to learn about the attribute of faithfulness. It's such an important lesson, and it's one that will benefit you throughout your life. Always try to be faithful, or true, to the teachings of the Bible and our Lord Jesus Christ."

"Okay, Mom," Madison said.

Her mom continued. "Several passages are very important, so pay close attention. The first is Hebrews 11:6. It says, 'And without faith it is impossible to please Him, for he who comes to God must believe that He is and that He is a rewarder of those who seek Him.' This passage tells us that to be a follower of Christ we must first believe that Jesus Christ exists. Once we believe this with all our heart, we must remain truthful to Him. But the first step is believing that Jesus Christ is real. Can you think of one example that shows you're faithful to Jesus?"

Madison thought for a moment and said, "Well, I pray every night before bedtime to thank Him for loving me."

Her mom smiled. "Yes, dear Madison, He does love you; that's a wonderful example. The next passage is from the book of Psalms 33:4, which says, 'For the word of the Lord is upright, and all His work is done in faithfulness.'"

Her mom explained this idea to Madison. "It's like the grapevine. We are rooted in Jesus as believers, and we must remember that He always has and always will be faithful and true to His word. It's important that we remember to thank the Lord for always being faithfulness to us."

Trish continued. "The last passage I'm going to read tonight is from the book of 1 Corinthians 4:2. This passage states, 'In this case, moreover, it is required of stewards that one be found trustworthy.' Do you know what *trustworthy* is, Madison?" her mom asked.

Madison answered eagerly, "I've got this one already! This is like you and Dad trusting me to tell you when my tummy hurts, no matter what."

"Well, it's kind of like that," her mother said, "but I'd like you to think about it like this—Jesus trusts us to learn about Him and His ministry. That's why He left the Bible for us to read. It's like our road map when we go on a trip, and if we follow what it says, it will lead us to Him. Since we believe in Him, He trusts us to be faithful with our knowledge, actions, and words. Being honest and true is being faithful," she explained.

"That makes sense. I can see how He would want us to be faithful with all that He's done for us. I have one question, Mom," Madison said.

"What's that?" her mom asked.

With a big sigh, Madison replied, "Will you and Dad tell me everything, no matter what Doc tells you?"

After a long pause, and fighting back tears, her mom said, "Yes, Madison, we will be honest with you. Now let's get to that bubble bath. You smell like the outdoors after playing in the clubhouse all afternoon."

Chapter 9
Gentleness

"Good morning, Mother," Madison said, walking into the kitchen. "I was wondering how many lessons are left to study the fruit of the Spirit."

Her mom looked up from her coffee and replied, "Well, we have two more; they are gentleness and self-control. Why?"

"Can we work on spelling and the next fruit of the Spirit before we go to see Lily and her mom?" Madison asked.

"I think we can do that," her mom replied. "Is there any particular reason you want to change the day?"

Madison replied, "Nope...Well, yes, but it's a surprise. I'm only telling you that because Jesus would want me to be honest."

Her mom smiled. "I'll tell you, Madison—you're just full of surprises. I love that about you, my sweet daughter. Let's get started in thirty minutes."

Trisha prepped the materials, wondering what Madison was planning. When Madison returned, she had dressed herself in a pair of her old jeans, a wrinkled T-shirt, and two crooked ponytails. "Oh my!" her mother said. "Are you dressed for anything special?"

Filled with pride, Madison said, "Yes. I got ready to go to the clubhouse with Lily later on. I figured this way I don't have to change to play outdoors."

Her mom chuckled. "Oh, I see. Well, we must focus on our studies now and talk about the outfit before we go. First things first. Let's discuss the next fruit of the Spirit, which is gentleness. We're going to learn about three passages in the Bible that teach us about this attribute. The first passage comes from the book of Galatians 6:1. It says, 'Brethren, even if anyone is caught in any trespass, you who are spiritual, restore such a one in a spirit of gentleness; each one looking to yourself, so that you too will not be tempted.'"

"What does that mean?" Madison asked.

"It means that everyone does things that are not right at some time or

another in his or her life," she explained. "Because you're a Christian, when you learn of someone's mistake, you should try to listen, understand, and help the person who has done wrong, because we all make mistakes along the way. The passage also cautions us about how we treat those who have made a mistake, and if we are not careful, we can be tempted to do something wrong as well."

"Let me see if I've got this," Madison said. "For instance, say Lily steals candy from the store without paying for it and gets caught. When her parents find out about it, they take her to apologize to the store owner and have her sweep the aisles as her punishment."

"You're doing great so far. Please continue," said her mother.

"Later, through the store window, I see Lily cleaning. If I begin to laugh at her, I am not acting with gentleness. If I go inside and give her a hug to make her feel better and reassure her that everything will be all right, then I am acting with gentleness. Is that right?"

Her mom replied, "Yes, Madison. That's a wonderful example of how we can show the Lord's gentleness toward others. Let's look at another passage. This one's from the book of Ephesians 4:2. It states, 'With all humility and gentleness, with patience, showing tolerance for one another in love.' Now, Madison, how would you apply this idea to the story you just told about Lily and the candy?"

"I guess the Bible is telling me to be kind to her, to listen carefully, and to give her a tight hug to let her know everything will be okay," Madison replied. "Mostly, I'd let her know I love her and so does Jesus."

"Wow! You're on top of things this morning," her mom said. "The final passage I'm going to read is also on gentleness. It comes from the book of Philippians 4:5, and it says, 'Let your gentle spirit be known to all men. The Lord is near.' How do you apply this to the same story about Lily and the candy?"

Madison considered it and said, "I suppose I could ask the store owner for a tissue to help dry Lily's tears, and by doing this in front of everyone in the store, I will show them Jesus lives in me and through my actions, which makes Him nearer to us."

Her mom responded with a big hug and kiss. "How on earth did I get such a wonderful and smart little girl?" she asked.

Madison giggled. "I guess you and Dad were good, so Jesus gave you me!"

"That was quite a lesson for today," her mom said. "I'm going to give Carol a call and let her know that we will be over shortly.

"Okay. Can I keep on this outfit?" Madison asked.

"The jeans are fine," her mother replied, "but I think we need to do something about your top. Go and pick out two more, and I'll be up to help you decide which one is best."

Madison couldn't wait to finish working on the clubhouse decorations with Lily. When she and her mom crossed the yard and swung open the gate, there stood Lily. She couldn't wait to get started either! "Come on! Come on! I've got something to show you, Madison!" Off they went to the clubhouse to play.

Trisha went in to sit with Carol and share information about how Christ has been the rock in her life, the rock that supports her and Roderick through Madison's illness.

Chapter 10
Have a Little Self-Control

Over the next few weeks, Madison and Lily grew to be the closest of friends. Each day, they would get together and work to make their clubhouse picture perfect. They had drawn many pictures, and they had even collected different items from their rooms to use for the decor that demonstrated the love of Jesus. Lily was humbled by the information Madison shared with her, and she was very happy with the theme they had chosen for their clubhouse. The two girls worked tirelessly to prepare activities that would entertain their families as they held an official open house of their new clubhouse.

After everything that Lily had learned from Madison about Jesus and the fruit of the Spirit, she was unsure about a couple of things. She had begun to say her prayers at night, but she wasn't saying them with her parents. She worried that Jesus couldn't hear her since she was talking to Him on her own. Madison reassured her that Jesus was available all the time and that she didn't need other people to be present for Jesus to listen to her. Lily felt better about that, but she was still concerned that her parents didn't seem to know about Jesus. So Madison and Lily decided to put together information on the fruit of the Spirit so that Lily's parents could learn about Jesus too. They would make programs and serve cookies and juice, just like the people did at Madison's church. They spent the rest of their time that afternoon using sparkles, markers, glue, and paint to create a wonderful program cover.

All too soon, it was time for the girls to go their separate ways for lunch and to finish their studies. Lily agreed to ask Levi to print the programs for them. Madison said she would get the snacks for their big event. The girls quickly set a time for the open house, exchanged a hug, and headed home to eat and relax for a little while before they continued their studies.

As they ate finger sandwiches, Madison asked her mother to explain the last fruit of the Spirit called self-control. Her mom began to explain. "Self-control is really important because the Lord gives us free will, which means that we get to choose to believe in Him and follow His teachings. Madison, the Bible teaches us to use self-control with our thoughts, speech, choices, and actions. The book of Titus 2:2 says, 'Older men are to be temperate, dignified, sensible, sound in faith, in love, in perseverance.' As we teach others, we should do it with respect, faith, and love, showing self-control for our actions."

"Is that like being polite?" Madison asked.

"In a way it is," her mom said. "But it's the reason you're being polite and deliberate with your decision that makes it a godly or ungodly choice. It's making a conscious choice to act appropriately because it's proper according to the teaching of Jesus Christ. Let me share another scripture with you. It's also in the book of Titus 2:12 and instructs us 'to deny ungodliness and worldly desires and to live sensibly, righteously and godly in the present age.'"

"Oh, I think I understand," Madison said. "This is very good information, but I'm getting a little tired. Mom, can I take a nap?"

"Sure. Are you feeling all right?" her mom asked.

Madison replied, "Yes. I'm just a little tired from all the excitement."

The next evening, Madison and her parents went to the Petersons' house for the big clubhouse opening. Lawn chairs and small end tables were set up in a semicircle facing the front of the clubhouse. A couple of multicolored balloons were tied to a stake in the ground at one corner of the clubhouse. They could hear the *bop-bop* of them bouncing on one another as they bobbed in the soft breeze.

Carol came out of the house with a big smile and said, "Welcome, welcome! I somehow became the hostess for tonight's event! We will have refreshments for you in a few minutes, so sit and relax while I steal Madison to help in the house." Trisha laughed and handed Madison a bag of treats to take into the house to Carol.

Soon it was the time for their program. The girls' parents sat in the chairs, as Levi and two of his friends sat on a red-and-black plaid blanket. Carol passed around trays with chocolate-chip cookies, slices of lemon cake, and foil-wrapped chocolates. Trisha handed out juice boxes and small bottles of water.

Once everyone had a snack, Madison said, "Here are your programs. Tonight, we want to share a message with you. We've both had cancer, and Jesus has taken it away. We believe that He did this for us because

He loves us so much. So if our cancer comes back, we will only call it the little *c*, because, from today on, the big *C* will stand for Christ, who is our Savior over all things. And His love is available for all of you too! We know this because of what He taught us through the fruit stories, starting with the vine."

Lily pointed toward the fence and said, "You see the grapevine along the fence?" They all responded that they did, so she continued. "The grapes need the grapevine for nourishment so they can grow. People are just like this, needing Jesus Christ for nourishment. He is the vine in our lives, and in order to grow in Spirit and love, we need Him and all the lessons He wrote for us in the Bible. We can do nine things to show that Jesus lives in our hearts once we accept Him as our Savior."

Madison stepped forward and said, "I will act as the kid who doesn't know Jesus as my savior, and Lily will be the one who does. Then you can see the difference. Here are the nine *att-ti-tues* of Christ."

"That's *attributes*, girls," Trisha called out.

"Right! What Mom said," Madison replied. Everyone began to chuckle. "The attributes are love, joy, peace, patience, goodness, kindness, faithfulness, gentleness, and self-control," Madison continued.

"When you love others, you act like this." Lily hugged Madison, who didn't hug her back.

"When you have joy, you act like this." Lily smiled as she danced in a small circle, saying, "I love Jesus. I love Jesus." Madison stomped her foot several times and folded her arms as if she was angry with the world.

"When you have peace, you act like this." Lily put her hands together as if to pray and gently smiled. Madison got a troubled look on her face and wiped her forehead in haste.

"When you have patience, you act like this." Lily turned to Madison, took her hand, and said, "Yes, dear child, you have been healed by the power of Jesus's love."

Madison said angrily, "Come on! Come on! You're taking too long."

"When you have goodness and kindness, you act like this." Lily said,

"Mama, may I help you carry your groceries to your car?"

Madison said, "I'm not carrying anything for her!"

"When you have faithfulness, you act like this." Lily knelt down on both her knees, bowed her head, and said, "Lord, I am so thankful for Your love and for bringing Madison into my life so that I can learn about You. Amen."

With tear-filled eyes, Madison said, "I can't do the opposite of that one, because I love Jesus too much to pretend not to be faithful to Him." She and Lily quickly hugged very tightly. Everyone softly cried tears of joy.

"Okay, so we're almost to the end," Lily told them all. "When you have gentleness, you act like this. Madison, sit here while I put a bandage on your cut knee."

Madison said, "Don't worry about it, crybaby."

"When you have a little self-control, you act like this," Lily continued.

Together, the girls said, "I'm not going to do the things that will dishonor Jesus because I love Him so very much. The end." They bowed and said, "Thank you for coming to our program. Now come have a look at our newly decorated clubhouse."

They all began to clap and cheer at the wonderful heartfelt demonstration of the girls' love for Jesus Christ. The adults stooped and, one by one, went into the clubhouse. They saw the walls decorated in many bright colors, with one oversized collage on the walls that had a long, winding grapevine. Attached to the vine were nine oversized grapes, each labeled with an attribute of the fruit of the Spirit. While the parents went in to look, Levi and his friends played music softly in the background.

Madison and Lily began to sing and hum the famous poem written in 1860 by Anna Bartlett Warner called "Jesus Loves Me." They sang proudly, "Jesus loves me, this I know, for the Bible tells me so."

Several of the neighbors heard the music and laughter and joined them all in the yard. Madison and Lily passed out extra programs to the neighbors as they came over.

"This is the happiest I've ever seen this community," Trisha said to Carol.

"What a wonderful thing you girls have done! Let's plan to do this again!"

"Absolutely, we will," Carol replied.

Trisha looked around at their husbands laughing, the kids joyful, and the friendly neighbors and said, "It's a blessing to have fruit in the Garden Clubhouse!"

Connect with Letitia

Email: Info@SelfDiscoverySolutions.com

Website: www.SelfDiscoverySolutions.com